ALIAS

Cliff O'Shea

GOD'S SECRET AGENT

BOOK 3

ALIAS

Cliff O'Shea

GOD'S SECRET AGENT
BOOK 3

PAUL THOMAS JORDAN

Principle Books Publishers

Scripture taken from the New King James Version.
Used by permission.

Cover and interior design by The Book Cover Whisperer: OpenBookDesign.biz

Published by Principle Books Publishers

First printing: November 2021

978-1-7331855-2-3 Paperback
978-1-7331855-3-0 eBook

Book available at amazon.com. eBook available on amazon.com, kobobooks.com, and the iBooks store.

To the memory of my sister,
Betty Jordan McClain, who walks
on golden streets in Heaven.

.

Contents

Foreword

"THIS IS THE THIRD installment of the wholesome tale of secret agent for the Kingdom of God, Cliff O'Shea. This story satisfies my curiosity about Jason and Jenny, only to leave me hungry for more!

"An exciting yet realistic tale that reflects the dearly held values of the Christian faith! Sometimes heart-wrenching and suspenseful, but always heart-warming!

"An entertaining story of a life lived in God's will. It's the ultimate fantasy of living in service to the Kingdom of God, not in a fantastical way, but in a way any man could imagine himself in.

"With quick segments of suspense that leave you satisfied by their resolution, it's a believable tale of a man and woman dedicated to serving God. I really wish there were more books in this sub-genre; it really feels like the Christian James Bond sometimes!

"Jason and Jenny are quickly becoming my beloved friends and mentors in my desire to truly walk with God!"

— **Garrison Pledger**

"THE THIRD CLIFF O'SHEA installment takes risks not seen before in the series. This is clearly a positive evolution in the story. I like watching Jason and Jenny realize that not every problem has the same solution. The ending leaves me eager for a fourth book."

— Zach Pledger

"I'M SO THANKFUL for this series. I like that not only is Jason doing God's work, but now he and Jenny are together seeking God for ways to help people. You can see the love they have for others through every encounter!"

— Rachel Pledger

"I REALLY DID ENJOY this book! There are a lot of exciting things in it and in the first two volumes. I'm now looking for volume four! I want to know what happens to some of the people I've met in these first three books!"

— Regina Williams Fitzpatrick

"THROUGH THIS SERIES, we get to learn along with Jason and Jenny how good God is. Through Scripture and the events in Jason and Jenny's lives, we are given example after example of God's overwhelming love for people. Jason and Jenny get to take part in God's plan for His people to have more than enough so they can prosper and thrive. We learn that when you focus on what you can do for the Lord and for others, you will also be taken care of and prosper in the process."

— Katherine Herbert

"WHEN READING ABOUT Jason and Jenny and the situations they keep finding around themselves, I am reminded of many situations I have come across that are very similar. I can see where Jason and Jenny always diligently seek to do God's will even when it is scary or when it seems that people will respond poorly. The outcomes shown in this book and in this series teach us that God has a purpose, as he tells us in the Bible, for us to follow His leadings. Even if things don't seem smooth or easy, He can use it.

"I love the idea of Cliff O'Shea and the abilities he has, through God, to help people. It's fun to read about him helping and imagining myself in the same situation. It makes me want to look out for those same scenarios in my own life and do what Jason does.

"I think it's important that real world issues are addressed in these books and backed with biblical ways on how to approach them.

"No matter your reading taste or genre preferences, there are lessons within these pages that will benefit anyone willing to listen. God can use Jason and Jenny to touch the hearts of Christians outside these pages!"

— **Lauren Lunney**

Preface

In Book One, we met a young teenager, Jason Lambert, who felt led by God to purchase an option for a piece of land. He then sold the option for a large sum of money and used the money to meet the needs of people God brought across his path.

He met a young girl named Jenny who captured his heart in a way he couldn't understand. He then spent almost five years searching for her. Only after he had turned his search over to God did he find her.

In Book Two, they both have graduated from college, and they are both working at the same High School, Jenny as a teacher and Jason as a Resource Person, as he helps the school solve some of its problems.

Before they got married, Jason had to reveal to Jenny that he is Cliff O'Shea, a fictitious character he invented so he could do his good deeds without being known.

At the end of Book Two, Jenny has told Jason that her 17-year-old student, Lilly Richards, is pregnant and her parents are pressuring her to have an abortion. Jenny wants to have Lilly come live with them and have the baby. She asks if Jason remembers her telling him about Lilly's situation.

ALIAS

Cliff O'Shea

GOD'S SECRET AGENT

BOOK 3

CHAPTER ONE

Life Is Sacred

"Sure. I remember," Jason answered.

"Would you be okay with Lilly coming to live with us?" Jenny asked.

"If that's what we need to do, I'm definitely okay with it. Let's pray about it, Jenny, and see if that's God's best plan for Lilly," Jason said as he took Jenny's hand to pray.[1]

After a minute or two of praying, Jason had a distinct feeling that he and Jenny needed to go talk with Lilly's parents. God had a bigger plan than just providing a home for Lilly.

"Jenny, I believe we need to go talk with Lilly's parents and help them see the error in what they're trying to have Lilly do. Do you know where she lives?"

"Out on Gypsum Road, in the country. She rides the school bus; says she's the last one to get off. Sometimes it's almost dark when she gets home. I don't know which house, though."

"It might be better if we talk to her parents when she's not home, so now might be a good time, before she gets there. We can start with the last house on Gypsum Road, since she says she's the last to get off the bus, and work our way back if that's not the right one. Is that okay with you, Jenny?" he asked.

"Jason, what if they get mad? What if they tell us it's not our business? That we have no right to interfere? I don't want what happened with Robert Shaw to happen again," Jenny said, nervously. "Couldn't we just tell Lilly she can come live with us? Maybe we wouldn't have to deal with her parents."

"I don't want any trouble, either, Jenny, but I believe God said we need to talk with them. He's concerned about them, too. If we're doing what He wants us to do, I believe He'll protect us. We can pray for His favor and for Him to direct what we say, so we can make them understand. Let's pray and ask if we're to go now."

As Jason prayed, Jenny became peaceful and began to smile. "Okay, Jason, I think you're right. We're to go now."

There were only three houses on all of Gypsum Road, all three on good-sized farms. They drove to the far end, to the last house, and turned into the long, winding driveway.

"If the bus lets her off at the road, Lilly has quite a walk to get to the house, doesn't she? Jenny noted. "I'm still a little nervous about this."

"Well, God said to do it, so we should be alright," Jason reassured her.

The house looked like a typical farmhouse, not poor-looking but not luxurious, either. A number of cows could be seen in the fenced yard just back of the house, and an older model pickup truck was parked at the end of the driveway in front of the house. Two dogs began barking as Jason and Jenny got out of the car.

Jenny plastered herself against the car, while Jason whistled and said, "Here, boy. Come on." Immediately, the barking stopped, and the dogs' tails began to wag as both came obediently to Jason.

Jenny just looked, amazed.

The barking had apparently alerted the man and woman inside, as the man opened the screen door, the woman looking out from behind him.

"Hello!" Jason called out. "Mr. Richards?"

"Yeah, that's me," the man answered, a little cautiously.

"I'm Jason Lambert. I work at Brookdale High School. This is my wife, Jenny. She's Lilly's teacher," Jason began.

"Has something happened to Lilly? Is she alright?" the woman stepped forward and asked, looking nervously from Jason to Jenny.

"Lilly's fine! We didn't mean to frighten you," Jason quickly explained. "We just wanted to talk with you for a few minutes, if that's okay. Would that be alright?"

"You sure Lilly's alright?" Her mother needed to be reassured.

"Yes, she's fine. We wanted to talk with you about her, though. Could we do that?" Jenny asked, smiling at the woman, trying to ease her distrust.

"Is this about her schoolwork? She's always been a pretty good student. Never had teachers come out to talk about her before." The woman still seemed cautious.

"Her schoolwork is just fine," Jenny assured her. "Lilly's been talking to me, Mrs. Richards, and she told me about the pregnancy."

With that, Mrs. Richards looked quickly at her husband, who suddenly frowned and looked away.

"Well, we could talk," Mrs. Richards said, looking at Mr. Richards again, but receiving no help from him. "James, let's go inside and talk to them. Please, can't we just talk to them?"

"Alright, I guess. Lilly shouldn't be telling this stuff to anybody. We didn't want anybody to know. She's bringing shame on the family," he answered. "Well, you already know. Come on inside."

Jenny didn't know where to start, so she was glad when Jason opened up with, "We know this is a difficult time for your family, Mr. Richards, and we want to help, if we can."

"I don't see how you can help. The deed's been done. Lilly's bringing shame to the family. We didn't raise her like this." The tension in Mr. Richards' voice was palpable. Mrs. Richards sat silent, with tears in her eyes.

"Mr. Richards, Mrs. Richards, Lilly's made one

mistake, but making her have an abortion would be a far greater mistake," Jason explained.

Jenny was praying silently.

"She told you about that, too, did she? Well, we're a Christian family. Having a baby before marriage is not supposed to be happening in a Christian family. She could have the abortion, and nobody would need to know about all of this. The way I see it, that's the only way out," Mr. Richards said.

"It's not a good way out, Mr. Richards. In fact, it's not a way out at all. Lilly would be hurt for the rest of her life if she went through with this. You say you're a Christian family, and I'm glad to hear that. Do you believe the Bible?" Jason asked.

"Of course I believe the Bible. What kind of question is that?" Mr. Richards asked, clearly irritated, pointing to the Bible laying on the coffee table in front of Jason.

"Mind if we read a verse from that Bible and see what you think?" Jason picked up the Bible and turned to Jeremiah 1:5.

"You read it, Mr. Richards, please." Jason held out the open Bible to him.

"Says *'Before I formed you in the womb,'*" Mr. Richards paused, thoughtful. He looked at Jason, then back down at the Bible. "*'I knew you.'*"[2]

"Who's saying that, Sir? Look at the verse right before that," Jason said, his voice full of compassion and patience.

"Says *'the word of the Lord'*. It's the Lord talking." Mr. Richards looked up at Jason, as understanding seemed to dawn on him. "It's the Lord saying that." He looked back at the Bible, as if to be sure he had read it right.

"Do you know what this is saying? God is saying this is already a baby, a person, no matter what you've been told about it being just a blob, a group of cells. It's a person," Jason continued. "Read the rest of verse five, if you will, Sir."

"*'Before you were born, I sanctified you; I ordained you a prophet to the nations,'*" he read slowly.

"God had ordained Jeremiah to be a prophet before he was born. He already has a plan for this baby's life, too.[3]Abortion would be taking that life. It would be murder.[4] This is your grandchild. It would be murdering your grandchild." As Jason said this, Mr. Richards covered his face with his hands and began sobbing, deep groans tearing out of his throat.

"Oh, God, what are we going to do?" Desperation in his voice, he cried out.

Mrs. Richards had been rocking her body back and forth, her face covered in tears as this conversation was taking place. Finally, she spoke. "We can't do this, James! We can't make Lilly murder a child! This is our grandchild!"

"I see we can't do it, Sue, but what are we to do? We'll be disgraced in front of everybody we know. Oh, God, why did this have to happen?" he cried out.

"I don't know why," Jason answered quietly, "but God will help all of you through this. We know someone who will help with the expenses—pay all of the doctor and hospital bills, buy baby furniture and clothes, anything Lilly needs, if that's a problem."

"If you don't want her to go to school, I can bring her assignments by every week so she won't fall behind," Jenny offered.

Mr. Richards was still holding the Bible. He looked down and read the verses again, silently this time. Then he closed the Bible and held it tight against his chest. "God, help us!" he whispered.

"God WILL help you," Jason said again. "Could we all just pray and agree that we want Him to take over and direct everything about this situation?"[5]

Without saying a word, both of Lilly's parents closed their eyes, tears still streaming down their faces, as Jason began to pray, "Father God, we know You're able to redeem any situation and bring great good out of it. You see the anguish these parents are feeling. I ask that You give them the peace that passes understanding[6], so that they can look forward to the birth of their grandchild with joyful anticipation of the child that is to come into their lives. Help Lilly as she goes through this pregnancy. Keep her healthy and safe. Oversee the development of this child that You already have a destiny planned for. Show Jenny and me all the ways we can be of help to this family.[7] We thank you for the gift of life. In Jesus' name we pray. Amen."

"Amen," Mr. Richards whispered.

As Jason and Jenny rose to go, Mrs. Richards grabbed Jenny and hugged her close. Mr. Richards cleared his throat and said, "I thank you for letting me see this in a different light. Those people who say life begins at first breath have it all wrong, according to what God says there. I wanted to believe them, but deep down, I guess I knew that was wrong. I just felt so desperate. I guess we're going to have to trust God and see this thing through. I, uh, believe you saved us from making a horrible mistake, so I thank you."

"Lilly will need medical attention to be sure this will be a smooth pregnancy and a healthy baby. Like I said, we know someone who will want to pay all of the expenses. Here's $500 to get her in to see the doctor and get things started," Jason said as he handed Mr. Richards the money.

"Remember, if you want Lilly to stop coming to school when she starts to show, I'll be happy to bring her assignments by. That way I'll get to stay in touch with her, too!" Jenny smiled at Mrs. Richards, who hugged her again.

On the way home, Jenny said, "I never dreamed that could go so well! You were so right, Jason. We needed to talk to her parents and help them see the right way to handle this. Now Lilly's family can be united around this baby. This is so much better than just having her come live with us, where she would have been estranged from her parents. I'm so relieved, and Jason, do you realize we may have saved a life? I mean, we would have tried to get Lilly to come live with us and have the baby rather than giving in to have an abortion, and I hope she would have agreed, but we can't be sure the pressure from her parents wouldn't have caused her to give in to them. Thank You, God, thank You, God! This is so much better!"

"Yep. God's ways really are higher than ours! That's why we always need to pray and ask for His guidance. [7] Maybe Lilly will have a different story to tell you at school tomorrow. We'll see how much Cliff O'Shea needs to be involved, and we'll stay involved, of course, to give moral support to the family. Speaking of guidance, maybe you could guide me to the restaurant where you would like to eat dinner, so we can celebrate a little for this good outcome!" Jason smiled, and began singing "God Is So Good."

.

CHAPTER TWO

False Imprisonment

M onday would be a holiday, so this would be a long weekend. Jason and Jenny hadn't been to Ermos in a while, so they decided to go visit his parents and help them celebrate their anniversary.

As soon as school was out on Friday, they were packed and ready, so they headed out. This had been a really good week at school, and both were looking forward to the weekend. They had only gone a few miles down the highway when two cars came flying around them at a high rate of speed.

"Wow! Somebody's in a real hurry! This highway's not straight enough for them to be racing like that!" Jason said, then he noticed something strange. The second car gained enough on the first to bump it in the rear on the left side, causing it to swerve to the right and almost go into the ditch.

"Whoa! This is not a race! That guy's trying to force the other one off the road! Quick, Jenny, call the Sheriff's Office and let's report this before something really bad happens!" Jason said, not taking his eyes off the road.

"Jason, I can't get a signal! Apparently, no service here! Oh, no! Just when we need it most!" Jenny exclaimed.

Jason was driving the speed limit, so the cars were quickly out of sight, as they had gone around a curve. As Jason and Jenny approached the curve, they saw dust filling the air. "Uh, oh! Something's happened!" Jason said, as they rounded the bend.

Then they saw it. The first car had flipped over and was down an embankment, its wheels still spinning in the air. The second car had stopped up the hill, and two men were getting out. "I guess they're going down to help, even though they probably caused this, judging by what we just saw," Jason thought as he pulled his car to the edge of the road and stopped.

Before he and Jenny could get out, he heard one of the men yelling toward the upturned car, "I hope you burn up!"

"They're not going to help at all!" Jason said, as he started down the embankment. "Jenny, go call for help! Get the Sheriff and an ambulance! Pop's Grocery Store is only about a mile further down the highway. Use their phone and get help!" Jason instructed over his shoulder.

"I don't want to leave you, Jason!" Jenny cried.

"I'll be alright! Just get help!" Jason called,

trying to keep his footing as he scrambled down the embankment.

"I love you, Jason!"

"I love you, too, now get going!" Jason answered.

"God, please help us!"[8] Jenny prayed as she quickly drove away, her heart beating so fast she could hardly breathe.

"You stay away from that car!" one of the men yelled to Jason. "That's my wife! You stay away!"

"Why aren't you helping her?" Jason responded as he continued toward the car.

"I'm telling you, stay away! You touch that car, and we'll beat you to a pulp!" The man threatened again and scrambled down to block Jason's path. Jason saw the second man just a few feet back, not saying anything but apparently backing up his buddy.

Jason could see the woman in the car crumpled in the seat, her head caught under the steering wheel, with the wheel pressing on her throat.

"She needs help, and she needs it right now!" Jason shoved past the man and reached for the door. When the man stepped in front and blocked his path, Jason used the palm of his hand and pushed hard, causing the man to stumble backwards and fall. Before the second man could get to him, Jason reached in the car and pressed the button under the steering wheel to change its position.[9] He heard the woman gulp in air as the wheel released her throat.

As the second man grabbed Jason from behind, Jason whirled around, breaking his hold, and with one quick blow, hit the man squarely in the nose. The man fell and rolled a couple of feet further down the embankment, out cold. By now the first man was up and yelling again, "I told you to stay away! Get your hands off that car!" He grabbed Jason's shirt but fell screaming to the ground from the Karate chop Jason gave his arm.

"You broke my arm!" He was writhing in pain as the ambulance arrived.

Jason watched as the ambulance workers quickly extracted the woman from the car, moved her into the ambulance, and sped away.

Jason looked up the bank and saw a Sheriff's car had arrived. "Thank God the Sheriff's here," he thought and began to climb back up the bank toward the Deputy who emerged from the car, straightening his gun belt as he looked around at the scene.

Jenny drove up just then and rushed down the bank to Jason.

"These guys"— Jason started to tell the Sheriff's Deputy, but was interrupted by the Deputy saying, "Well, hello, Cuz. What happened here?" He was looking past Jason and speaking to the first man.

"This man ran me and Rebecca off the road. My buddy here came along just in time to help us, or at least he was trying to when this guy hit him in the nose and knocked him out. I think this guy broke my arm, too." He grimaced and groaned to show his pain as he said this.

"Wait a minute!" Jason interjected. "He's lying!" Jason tried to begin again.

"You calling my cousin here a liar?" the Deputy stepped up close to Jason's face, threatening.

"We were trying to help that woman!" Jenny cried.

"You stay out of this, little lady. I'll handle this." He turned back to Jason and said, "Put your hands behind you back. You're going to jail."

"No!" Jenny yelled. "No! You've got the wrong guy! Jason was helping the woman!"

"I told you to be quiet, little lady. Want me to arrest you, too?" as he put the handcuffs on Jason.

By now Jenny was crying.

"It'll be alright, Jenny. We'll get this straightened out. Call my mom and tell her what happened and where we are," Jason said over his shoulder as the Deputy pushed him and they went up the bank to the patrol car.

Jenny followed behind as the patrolman took Jason to jail in the small town of Eastman. She found a phone and called Mrs. Lambert, crying as she tried to explain what had happened. "Jenny, I'll be there as soon as I can. Stay there at the jail so you'll know where Jason is. I'll get Mr. Allewine, too. Hang in there!"

In less than an hour, Mrs. Lambert was there,

though it had seemed like an eternity to Jenny. Mrs. Lambert and Jenny were allowed to talk to Jason and hear his side of the story, then Mrs. Lambert asked to speak to the Sheriff.

Jenny sat in the hallway, waiting for Mr. Allewine, who had not yet arrived.

As Mrs. Lambert was escorted into the Sheriff's office, she noticed the nameplate on his desk: Sheriff Allen Moreland. "Thank you for seeing me, Sheriff Moreland. There has been a grave mistake here. My boy would never do what you are accusing him of. He was trying to help that woman."

"Sorry, Ma'am, but I have to believe what my officers tell me. That's all I have to go on," the Sheriff explained. "The Judge will make the final decision Monday morning."

"Monday morning! You mean to keep him here till Monday morning? Can't I get him out on bail?" Mrs. Lambert asked.

"No, Ma'am." The Sheriff explained. "If that woman dies, he'll be charged with murder. No bail for that."

"But my son didn't do it! I would stake my life on it!"

"Mrs. Lambert, there's nothing I can do. Now, if you'll excuse me, I'm very busy." With that, the Sheriff began shuffling some papers on his desk, making sure Mrs. Lambert knew the interview was over and she should leave.

Mrs. Lambert found Jenny outside, still crying, and

told her what the Sheriff had said. She sat beside her and took her hand. "Jenny, let's pray. God knows the truth, and He can fix this."

Then she began to pray. "Father God, You tell us to come boldly before Your throne to find help in time of trouble.[8] Well, we're in trouble here, and we're coming for that help. You know how wrong this situation is. Until we can get Jason out, we need You to protect him from harm while he's here. We even ask You to bring good out of all of this somehow.[10] Show us what all we need to be doing. In the meantime, we're putting all our trust in You."

Jenny felt a little better, but said, "I can't stand the thoughts of Jason having to spend the weekend in jail. Let me talk to the Sheriff. Nobody has heard my side of the story."

"I don't think it will do any good, Jenny, but we can try."

"Well, at least I will feel better if I know he's been told the truth. The Deputy wouldn't even let Jason or me talk," Jenny said.

Mrs. Lambert led the way back to the Sheriff's office and knocked on the door.

"Come in!" the Sheriff said.

When he saw it was Mrs. Lambert again, he said in exasperation, "I told you, Mrs. Lambert, I can't do anything for him. The Judge will decide on Monday."

Jenny spoke up and asked, "Can't I at least tell you

what really happened? I'm Jason's wife. I was there! You need to hear the truth."

The Sheriff sighed. "Go ahead, if it makes you feel any better, but like I told Mrs. Lambert, I have to believe what my officers tell me."

"Well, they've obviously told you wrong this time. Jason and I were headed to Ermos to see his parents when two cars came flying by us. For a second, we thought they were racing, but then we saw the second car bump the first car, trying to push it off the road. They went around a bend and out of our sight till we got around the bend, too. That's when we saw the first car upside down and down the embankment and the second car pulled over. I tried to call for help but couldn't get any service on my cell phone, so Jason sent me to Pop's Grocery Store to call for help. I got back just after the ambulance did and at the same time as the Deputy. The ambulance took the woman, but then the Deputy arrested Jason!" At this she broke down crying again.

The Sheriff looked uncomfortable and shuffled the papers on his desk, moved his coffee cup, and cleared his throat.

Before he could say anything, Jenny started up again. "You've got the wrong man, Sheriff! Jason and I were helping! How can you lock him up for that? That man in the other car was yelling out to the car down the embankment, 'I hope you burn up!' It was obvious he wasn't going to help. Your Deputy wouldn't even let us tell him what had happened! He wouldn't let us talk!"

"I'm sorry, Miss, but like I said, I have to believe my officers until it's proven otherwise. Your saying this is not proof. It's just your word against somebody else's. I'm not the Judge. The Judge will hear the story on Monday and make a decision."

"Think, Sheriff, please! Would I have gone to the trouble to call for an ambulance and to call your office if we had been the ones to run that car off the road?"

"Sorry, Miss, but this doesn't change anything. Now, that's all the time I have for this. Please excuse me." With that he looked down and began studying a paper on the desk.

Jenny sighed and looked at Mrs. Lambert, who was just shaking her head. The two of them slowly turned and walked out the door.

They both felt a little better when Mr. Allewine arrived about five minutes later. After he had heard the full story from Jenny, he knocked on the Sheriff's door and asked to be allowed to speak with Jason. The Sherriff instructed a Deputy to take Mr. Allewine back to Jason's cell.

He found Jason deep in a conversation with a man whose feet and legs were hanging off the top bunk and who was listening intently. Jason looked up, and relief spread across his face as he saw his lawyer. He quickly told his account of the incident, then suggested that Mr. Allewine go immediately to the hospital and see if he could speak with the injured woman. He would find her story would match Jason's, plus he might find out what the chase was all about.

After getting the woman's name and the name of the hospital from the Deputy, Allewine told Jenny and Mrs. Lambert what he was about to do. Jenny wanted to go with him, but Mrs. Lambert decided she should stay there, just in case the Sheriff decided to move Jason or make some changes they wouldn't know about. She didn't feel they could trust the Sheriff to keep them informed.

Mr. Allewine and Jenny found Rebecca Walker in room 309 at Memorial Hospital. They had expected to find a Deputy guarding her room, but no one was in sight. They knocked and when she answered, Jenny stuck her head in the door first and said, "My husband and I saw the accident. I'm Jenny. I went to call for help while Jason, my husband, went down the hill to where your car was. He's the one who released the steering wheel off your neck. May we come in and talk with you?"

"Yes! Yes, of course. Do come in. Thank you for stopping to help." Rebecca Walker sat up in bed and appeared to be alright, except for her tear-streaked face and a red stripe across her neck. She reached out toward Jenny, who took her hand and smiled to put her at ease.

"This is Mr. Allewine, our lawyer. When I called for help, the Sheriff sent a Deputy out. One of the two men in the other car told him we had run you off the road. The Deputy called the man his cousin and obviously believed him. He wouldn't let my husband or me tell our side of the story. He arrested Jason for attempted murder, and the Sheriff says he will have to stay in jail over the weekend until the Judge sets the bail."

"Oh, no! What can I do?" Rebecca exclaimed. "That was my ex-husband who ran me off the road. He's the one who should be arrested for attempted murder!"

"Mrs. Walker, can we get your statement and have you sign it so we can take it back to the Sheriff and to the Judge, if necessary?" Mr. Allewine asked.

"Of course! I'll do anything to help. Jason saved my life! I don't know how I'll ever be able to thank him enough!" She looked helplessly at Jenny as tears rolled down her cheeks. "Please let me tell what happened and use it any way you can."

"I'll get some paper from the nurse, and we'll get your statement." With that, Mr. Allewine stepped out of the room.

"I can't believe they arrested your husband! I'm so sorry. If you hadn't stopped to help, I guess I'd be dead," Rebecca sobbed.

Jenny said, "I'm glad we were there at the right time so that you're okay, even with all the trouble."

Mr. Allewine came back in with a clipboard and several sheets of paper. "I'll record your story in a video on my phone, but I'd like to have a written account for you to sign, too, if you don't mind."

Rebecca began to tell her sad story. "My name is Rebecca Walker. That man who tried to, I mean who ran me off the road, was my ex-husband. We have been divorced for two years. I have a good job that pays pretty well, and Cecil thought he could get money from me."

"So his name is Cecil Walker?" Mr. Allewine asked.

"No, it's Cecil Evans. I went back to my maiden name after the divorce. Anyway, he was drinking pretty heavily when he came by today. He told me he had been fired and he wanted me to pay him $700 a month until he could get another job. I told him I couldn't do that and to please leave. He pulled out a pistol and shot near me. He missed me. He said he didn't mean to shoot, that the gun just went off, but he was grinning as he said it. I know he wanted to scare me. Well, he sure did. I thought he might kill me. When he started looking around the house for money, I ran through the kitchen where my purse and keys were, grabbed them and was out the door and almost to my car before he came to the door and saw me. I got in my car and drove off as fast as I could. He and that other man got in his car and started chasing me. I tried to get away, but they kept up. They bumped me twice before the time they pushed me off the road. I think they were really trying to kill me!" With that she broke down sobbing again.

Jenny put her arm around her and patted her back. She couldn't think of anything to say, Rebecca's story was so sad.

Mr. Allewine had written the important facts of the story while it was being recorded, then let Rebecca look it over and sign it. "Would you swear out a warrant on Cecil?" he asked.

"Yes! Right now! I'll be glad to!" she answered.

"We'll tell the Sheriff and have them take care of it. This video and signed statement should let us get Jason out of jail. Thank you for your cooperation, Mrs. Walker," Allewine said.

Jenny hugged her and thanked her, then left wondering if the poor woman was safe, even there in the hospital, since the man who had tried to kill her was still on the loose.

When Jenny and Allewine arrived back at the Sheriff's office and jail, Mrs. Lambert jumped up from her chair and said, "A Deputy just came in and told the Sheriff that the woman will be okay!"

"She will be, and she is, okay," Allewine assured her. "We have her signed statement and a video, which I'm about to show to the Sheriff. This should get Jason off the hook completely."

As Jenny shared with Mrs. Lambert all that Rebecca Walker had told them, Allewine knocked on the Sheriff's door and entered. Within minutes he was back out with a big smile on his face.[11]

"That did it. He had no choice but to drop the charges against Jason. This Deputy is going back with me to get Jason out now," as he gestured toward a Deputy who was smiling and swinging a large set of keys. "We won't be long!"

As he headed back toward Jason's cell, following the Deputy, he could hear big sighs of relief from Jenny and Mrs. Lambert, as they sat down to wait, thinking they would see Jason at any moment. To their surprise, Allewine came back alone, with a smile on his face.

"You won't believe this," he said. "Jason asked me to give him a few more minutes! He's talking to the guy who's in the cell with him. Nobody but Jason would want to stay in jail a few minutes longer! He told me to take you two somewhere to get something to eat. I'll be happy to do that, if you'll go."

Jenny and Mrs. Lambert looked at each other in surprise. "Well! I don't guess we have any choice but to give him a few more minutes. What can he be thinking?" Mrs. Lambert asked.

"I don't think I want to leave," Jenny said. "You don't know what might happen. I'd rather stay here."

"So would I," Mrs. Lambert said. "Whatever he has in mind can't take too long."

"Okay, we'll all stay," Allewine agreed and pulled up a chair to sit with them.

After about twenty minutes, Mr. Allewine said, "I can't wait any longer! I want to get him out of here. I'm going back to see if he's ready." With that he got the Deputy with the keys, and they disappeared down the hall.

Jason had a big smile on his face. "I'm ready now!" Then he turned to shake hands with the man sitting on the bunk. "This was a really important decision you just made, Carl. I'm going to get you a Bible, then you need to find a Bible-believing church so you can grow. Your life's going to be very different from here on out. I'll stay in touch."

Allewine looked and saw tears streaming down the man's face. A bit puzzled, he looked back at Jason and saw he had a big smile spreading from ear to ear.

The Deputy unlocked the cell door and let Jason out. As soon as he and Mr. Allewine were out of earshot, he whispered, "Carl there just met Jesus! I couldn't leave until he had made that decision."[12]

"You're something else, Jason Lambert. I'm pretty impressed with you! Now, let's go talk to the Sheriff about that Deputy who arrested you," Allewine said, as he led the way to the Sheriff's office. "We can file a suit on him for False Imprisonment. We won't sue him for any money if the Sheriff will fire him. He shouldn't be an officer of the law."

At Allewine's request, the Sheriff called for the Deputy who had arrested Jason to come to his office. After about ten minutes, he arrived. He looked very surprised to see Jason in the Sheriff's office rather than in a cell.

"Well, Luther. Seems the lady in the car has a different story to tell than the one you told me. What do you have to say for yourself?"

"Yeah, Sheriff, I was just about to come in and tell you that I had found out some new facts," Luther lied and shuffled his feet, a very different person from the over-confident, arrogant person Jason and Jenny had encountered on the hillside.[13] He was clearly intimidated by the Sheriff, and no doubt his guilty conscience had him disturbed. He kept his eyes averted from Jason and Mr. Allewine.

"New facts, huh? Why didn't you get all the facts before you arrested this man? And Jason here says you called one of the men 'Cuz.' Was one of them your cousin? Seems like you willingly overlooked what your cousin had done and arrested the wrong man without getting any facts at all. That's not the way we apply the law. You know that."

"Yeah, Sheriff. Cecil Evans is my cousin, and I believed what he told me. I made a mistake, I guess. Won't happen again, Sheriff," Luther mumbled, twisting his hat in his hand and shifting from one foot to the other.

He clearly wanted this over with. He looked like he might bolt for the door any minute.

"A mistake, huh? Seems like you've made a string of 'em lately. Mr. Lambert's lawyer here wants to file a suit against you for Wrongful Imprisonment. Says he won't ask for any money if I relieve you of duty and kick you off the Force. We'll have to follow procedures to see about that, but for now, I'll need you to give me your gun and badge, and the keys to the cruiser. I'll get somebody to give you a ride home." The Sheriff sounded like a different man from the one who just a couple of hours ago had told Jenny and Mrs. Lambert, "I have to believe my officers."

When the gun, badge, and keys were on the Sheriff's desk and Luther was out the door, Mr. Allewine said, "We'll be in touch, Sheriff, to see how you handle this. We'll file that suit if we need to, and I'll talk to some of my friends at the State Law Enforcement Department and get them to look into how this office is run, if we find we need to. Meanwhile, some of your Deputies have some work to do to round up Cecil Evans and his buddy."

"Right you are! We'll get that warrant, with Mrs. Walker's agreement, and get Evans and his friend rounded up." Now the Sheriff sounded as humble as Luther had been. "I appreciate your getting the straight story to me," he added, as he nodded to Jason.

When they were in the hall, Allewine told Jason that he would check and make sure the Sheriff followed through. Jason thanked him, shook his hand, gave him a big smile, and said, "Send me your bill! Jenny and I have a weekend to celebrate an anniversary with my parents."

CHAPTER THREE

Good Medicine

By the time Jason, Jenny, and Mrs. Lambert arrived in Ermos, it was a little late to go to the upscale restaurant where Jason had made a reservation to celebrate his parents' anniversary. He called and changed the reservation for the following night instead. They went through a drive-through and picked up sandwiches after calling and checking with Mr. Lambert to be sure he was okay with the change in plans. As they sat around the kitchen table, they filled Mr. Lambert in on all the day's happenings. He sure got an ear full. What a day it had been!

Then Jenny and Jason were glad to be able to go to bed early. Their bedtime prayers were longer than usual this night, they had so much to thank God for.[14]

The next day, Jason helped his dad cut up a huge limb that had fallen from a tree in the front yard and was now blocking the driveway. They stacked the pieces by the curb with a note that anyone who wanted it could have free firewood.

Mrs. Lambert got Jenny to go with her so they both

could get a pedicure, then they came home and watched a Hallmark movie together while Jason helped his dad outside. Mrs. Lambert knew Jenny really needed to de-stress, and she admitted that she needed a bit of relaxation herself.

Late that afternoon, they went to the restaurant to celebrate an anniversary AND celebrate Jason being released from jail. Jenny was still a bit shaken from all that had happened and was glad they had the anniversary to celebrate. She asked the Lamberts to tell her how the two of them had met, what they thought of each other at the first meeting, how long before they knew they were in love, how long before they married, etc. It was a wonderful time for all four of them.

As they were finishing dessert, Mrs. Lambert suddenly remembered something she had been meaning to tell Jason. "Jason! I can't believe I keep forgetting to tell you this. Our Ken Robertson has become quite a celebrity lately!"

"Who is Ken Robertson?" Jenny asked.

"A wonderful person who lived on the other side of us from the Shaws. He used to babysit with me some. Actually, I prefer to say we hung out together rather than saying he babysat me. I was a little old for 'babysitting.' I must have been about nine when he moved in next door. What has he done to become a celebrity, Mom?" Jason then asked.

"Well, that trendy restaurant over on Main Street

called the 'Do-Wop' has a rather large meeting room on the right side. A while back, they started having Karaoke nights, and once a month they allow story-tellers, poets, or comedians to be the entertainment. We knew Ken always had a keen sense of humor, but he has just blossomed as a comedian. He draws quite a crowd when people know he'll be speaking. They don't start until about an hour from now, so if you wanted to, you two could still catch him tonight. He may not be the entertainment for another couple of months after this."

"Ken a comedian!?" Jason laughed at the thought. He turned to Jenny and explained. "He has always had a wonderful sense of humor and could always see the bright side of everything. He had been a widower for a couple of years before he moved next door, and unfortunately, they had no children. I guess that was why he always seemed to enjoy having me around. He had just retired from his job as a Civil Engineer. He is a brilliant man."

"Sometimes it happened that Jason's dad and I both had to work a little late or got caught in traffic, if you can believe we ever have traffic jams in such a small town. Anyway, we could always call Ken and ask if he would watch out for Jason until we got home. He acted like he loved doing it," Mrs. Lambert explained.

"He would be outside waiting for me when I got off the school bus, or a few years later, when I rode my bike home. 'How about come hang out with me,' he would say and explain that my parents would be a little late. He would make us both a snack, then ask me to tell him about my day. He never seemed to get tired of my description of an ordinary day. Then he would tell me something about the things he had done as a Civil Engineer. I'm sure he had to dumb it down a lot to make it clear to a kid, but it was fascinating."

"Do you want to go see him tonight? It sounds like it would be fun, and I would love to meet him," Jenny said.

"Why not, Jason? We're finishing up here, and I know he would love to see you," Mr. Lambert offered. "Linda and I can find a movie or ballgame to watch on TV at home."

"Movie!" Mrs. Lambert inserted quickly, causing laughter around the table.

Ken had already begun to speak when Jason and Jenny arrived. They could hear the laughter before they ever entered the restaurant.[15] The room to the left was filled with people seated at tables and eating. Not a table was empty. "The restaurant must be doing well," Jason thought, as he told the hostess they were just there for the entertainment, and didn't need to be seated at a table.

The room to the right was filled with three rows of chairs arranged in a semi-circle, with the speaker seated at the front. As they entered, they found only three chairs were empty, all three on the back row and no two of them together. As they looked around, deciding what to do, a couple moved down one seat, leaving two together for Jason and Jenny. Jason mouthed "Thank you" and motioned Jenny to a seat, just as he heard, "Well, well, well. Sorry to interrupt what I was saying, but there's my old friend Jason Lambert. How're you doing, Jason? Come to hang out with me for a while?"

Jason smiled and nodded to Ken, just as happy to be together as Ken obviously was.

Let's see now. Where was I? Oh, yeah. Now, I don't remember where I heard this story, so I don't know who to give credit to. Like I said, this man was waiting outside of a restaurant, waiting for his wife to join him. He spotted a bench and thought he'd sit to wait. Someone had left a newspaper on the seat, and not thinking, the man sat right down on it.

It hadn't been five minutes before another man arrived to wait outside, too. He just looked at the first man for a minute, then asked, "Are you reading that paper?"

"Yep. Sure am. Matter of fact, I was just about to turn the page." With that, he got up, turned the page, then sat back down on the paper.

The crowd roared with laughter, Jason and Jenny joining in.

Ken then proceeded to share tale after tale, making

the crowd of people hold their sides from laughing so hard.

"He is really good!" Jenny whispered to Jason. "He would be worth making the trip back down here anytime he's appearing."

"He IS good!" Jason answered. "I never knew he was this funny. This has to be good medicine for these people.[15] No wonder he draws a crowd!"

I'll give credit for this one to my man, Billy Graham. Heard him tell this. Teacher wanted the class to find out what country of origin their family was from, so she told them to ask their parents where they came from.

Bobby asked his mother, "Where did I come from?"

"The stork brought you," his mother answered, hoping there would be no further questions.

Bobby thought about that for a while, then he went to his grandmother and asked, "Where did my mother come from?"

"The stork brought her," Grandmother answered, hoping there would be no further questions.

Bobby had one more source he could check, so he called up his Great Grandmother and asked, "Where did Grandmother come from?"

"The stork brought her," was the answer.

Bobby wrote his answer for his teacher: "I

don't know where we came from, but there hasn't been a natural birth in our family for three generations."

Laughter from the crowd, then Ken continued.

Billy Graham said one time he had arrived in a new town where he was to preach in a tent meeting. He wanted to send a card home to his family. Out on the street, he asked a young boy for directions to the Post Office. The boy told him how to get there, then Billy told the boy he would be preaching that night in the tent that was just a couple of blocks away.

"Why don't you come tonight and hear my sermon? I'll tell you how to get to Heaven," Billy said.

"I don't know," the boy answered. "You don't even know how to get to the Post Office."

More laughter.

While I'm telling Billy's stories, he gets credit for this one, too. A man came upon a drunk standing under a street light, looking on the ground. "What are you looking for?" the man asked. "I lost my wallet," the drunk answered. "Did you lose it here?" "No. About a half a block up the street." "Then why aren't you looking for it there?" the puzzled man asked. "There's no street light up there," was the answer.

Ken waited for the laughter to stop.

A man decided to go skydiving for the very first time. He went to the place where he could hire the plane and somebody to go up and get him suited up for the jump. When the door of the plane opened and he looked down at the ground so far away, he got pretty scared.

The man who was suiting him up said, "I'll tell you what. We'll give you two parachutes. When you pull the ripcord on the first one, if it doesn't open up, just pull the cord on the second one. Then there will be a man with a jeep on the ground to pick you up."

With the two chutes on his back, he got up his courage and jumped out of the plane. He pulled the cord for the first chute, and nothing happened. Didn't open up. So, he pulled the cord on the second one, same thing. Didn't open up. Disgusted, he said, "I bet the man with the jeep won't be there, either."

Gasping, then laughter.

Saw this statement the other day from a man named Lance Hall: "Lance is a pretty uncommon name these days, but in medieval times, people were named Lance a lot."

Snickering.

After we graduated from High School, my buddy Johnny and I thought we'd go down to Florida, go to the beach, look around, maybe find us a job down there and stay a while. Soon as we got into Florida, we saw a sign, "Orange juice. All you can drink for 15 cents."

"Boy, that's a good deal," we decided, so we whipped the car right in to the parking lot, went inside, both paid our 15 cents and got our cup of juice. We drank it right down, then set our cups down on the counter and said we were ready for more.

"That'll be 15 cents," the man said.

"But your sign said 'All you can drink for 15 cents.'"

The man pointed to our empty cups, "Yep. That's all you can drink for 15 cents."

It took a few seconds for the audience to catch on, then roars of laughter.

Two blondes were in an airplane along with about 20 other people. The plane had four engines. About 30-40 miles out, the pilot came on the speaker and announced: "Ladies and gentlemen, one of our four engines just went out. There's no cause for concern, as we have three others. Just letting you know that this will cause us to be about a half hour late. Continue to enjoy your flight."

A while later, he came on the speaker again to announce: "Ladies and gentlemen, I need to let you know that a second engine has gone out, so now we will be an hour late. No cause to worry. We still have two engines. Continue to enjoy your flight."

The two blondes were a little upset but settled back down. Unfortunately, the pilot had to come back on the speaker again to report a third engine had gone out, and they would be an hour and a half late. The first blonde said in exasperation, "If the fourth engine goes out, we'll be up here all day."

When the laughter quieted down, Ken continued.

I don't mean to pick on blondes. They just give me lots of material. For instance, two blondes ran into a building. Looks like the second one would have seen it.

Snickering.

Unfortunately, this next scenario really happened, much to my chagrin. I must have been in the seventh grade. We still had cloakrooms back then where we hung up our coats and caps. I had a new cap that I was very proud of, so I wore it to school. At the end of the day, I went to the cloakroom to get it before going home. I was shocked when it wasn't there. I went back and looked in my desk and under my desk. Finally, I went up and told the teacher that my cap was missing. Teacher quieted the class down and asked them all to help me look for my cap. After several minutes of the class searching, a boy in the corner said, "It's on his head!" I'm sad to say, it was. It was there all the time. I didn't know whether to be happy that we had found it, or just embarrassed at the stupidity of it all.

That was not as bad as the next true story.

My friend Gladys told me this. It really happened to her. She was selling insurance and going door-to-door. When she knocked on this particular door, a little girl with a sucker in her mouth came and answered the knock. Gladys asked if her mother was home and could she come in to see her. Little girl didn't say a word, just opened the door and motioned Gladys in to the living room. Little girl motioned to the couch. Gladys thought she was inviting her to sit down on the couch, although it was covered with blankets and looked a bit lumpy. "Oh, well, nowhere else to sit," she thought. So, she sat down on the couch and waited. And waited. And waited. The little girl had gone into another room, to get her mother, Gladys thought.

The little girl finally came back into the room, and Gladys asked, "Where's your mother?"

"You're sittin' on her," was the answer. Gladys didn't sell any insurance at that house.

Ken continued next with a chicken story.

Farmer Jones had a wife and one son. The three

of them all liked a fried chicken leg for dinner, and they had plenty of chickens, as that was mostly all they raised. The problem was, all three wanted a leg, and every chicken only had two. If they killed and cooked two chickens, one leg would be wasted and that was also a waste of chickens.

To solve the problem, Farmer Jones began to breed three-legged chickens. Pretty soon, three-legged chickens were all he had.

Neighbor Smith was driving down the road one day and noticed a chicken running along beside his car. The chicken was keeping up with him! He sped up until finally he was doing 60 miles an hour. He looked out the window, and sure enough, the chicken was right with him. Suddenly the chicken cut off and ran to the Jones' farm.

Farmer Smith kept going, but the next day the same thing happened, so he thought he'd better find out what was going on. He went to talk with Farmer Jones. "Man, I've seen two chickens that could run as fast as my car, and they both turned into your farm. What's going on?"

Jones explained that they needed three chicken legs for each family member to have one, so they started breeding three-legged chickens.

"Well, are they any different to eat? Do they taste the same?" Smith asked.

"Don't know," Jones answered. "We can't catch 'em."

My buddy Dick Hardwick told me about an experience he had. He was staying in a nice hotel on a visit when the Housekeeper knocked on the door to his room. He said, "Yes?"

Housekeeper asked, "Can I come in and clean up?"

He said, "Okay," and opened the door. She came in, took a shower, and left.

He said someone asked him the other day, "Have you lived here your whole life?" "Not yet," was his answer.

I never cease to be amazed at some people. At a very busy spot on the highway, a sign was posted: DEER CROSSING. A lady called the highway department very irate. "That's a very busy part of the road. You should know better than to have the deer crossing at that place."

Preacher was preaching a sermon on Heaven. He told the congregation, "If you want to go to Heaven, stand up!" Everybody stood up but one old man. Preacher looked at him a minute, then out of concern, asked, "Don't you want to go to Heaven when you die?" "When I die, yeah. I thought you were gettin' up a load to go now."

I'll close with this story about motivation you need to hear. A guy had been drinking heavily at the bar, when he decided to start for home. He was too drunk to drive, so he started walking.

He decided to take a shortcut through the graveyard. It was pitch-black dark. Couldn't see a thing. Unfortunately for him, a grave had just been dug for a burial the next day. Before he knew what had happened, he fell into the hole.

The sides were straight up. He couldn't get a foothold or a handhold anywhere. He tried and tried until he was exhausted. He finally sat down against the back side, deciding to wait till morning when surely someone would come by and rescue him.

In the meantime, another guy also left the bar, too drunk to drive. He decided to take the same shortcut. Sure enough, he fell into the same hole. Like the other guy, he clawed and clawed at the side but couldn't get a foothold or a handhold so he could climb up. In that pitch-black dark, the first man said, "You can't get out."

He did.

Ken finally said, "That's all folks. Thank you for coming! Next time, I'll tell you why the chicken crossed the road!"

When the people got up, laughing and talking to each other as they began to leave, Jason and Jenny headed to the front.

"Well, well, well. How's my boy?" Ken said as he

grabbed Jason for a bear hug. "This pretty thing must be Jenny." He bowed a bit, took her hand, and kissed it.

"I've heard ALL about you from the Lamberts. Sorry I was traveling and didn't make it to your wedding. I hear Jason's a lucky boy."

"Lucky doesn't come close," Jason said. "Man, this was good tonight!" he exclaimed. "You've always been good with humor, but this was GOOD!"

"Thank you, Jason. Glad you enjoyed it. Let's go over to the restaurant side and get some sweet tea. Need to wet my whistle. Mostly, I want to catch up on what's been going on with you two."

The restaurant was open for another hour, so they used it up, talking and laughing. Ken still had that way with humor, even when he wasn't performing. Jason and Jenny told him what had happened on their way down to Ermos, then they talked a lot about the school.

"The perfect way to cap off our weekend before going home tomorrow," Jason thought.

CHAPTER FOUR

Leroy, Grandpa, and Shirley

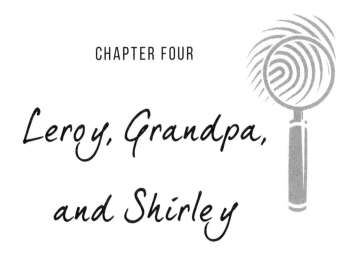

Jason and Jenny went to church with his parents, afterwards they all went to lunch, then Jason and Jenny left for home. It was still pretty early when they arrived in Brookdale, so Jason told Jenny he'd like to go by and check on JD and Leroy Adams, just to see how they were doing. He hadn't heard anything from them in quite a while.

On the way, Jason told Jenny all about how he had met the old gentleman and his grandson, Leroy. He had told her a little about it when he had first revealed to her that he was Cliff O'Shea, showing her the kind of things God had him do with the money he had in the O'Shea account. O'Shea was still paying for Leroy's self-defense classes,[16] but he hadn't had any personal contact with him or the grandfather in a while.

When they arrived, the grandfather was sitting on

the front porch in the swing. Jason saw him squint as he looked at the two of them getting out of the car. When they got closer, he shouted out, "Jason Lambert, is it really you? Bless God, it is! And who is this pretty young thing?"

Jason smiled as he grabbed the old man's hand. "This is my wife, Jenny, and you're right, she IS a pretty young thing, inside and out." Then he said, "Jenny, this is one of the nicest people you could ever hope to meet on this earth, JD Adams."

Jenny smiled and held out her hand. "I've been looking forward to meeting you, Mr. Adams. Jason has told me a little about you, but I'm hoping to know more." Then she sat down by him on the swing.

"Sit down, Jason, sit down. There's room for all three of us." He slid over, and Jenny slid with him so Jason could sit, too.

"I can't tell you how much I've enjoyed this porch and this swing Mr. O'Shea gave us! Me and Leroy sit out here and talk almost every afternoon, even when it's raining. I love the smell that comes up from the earth when it first starts to rain. Rain's a gift from God, you know. Just cause the Bible says God lets it rain on the just and the unjust, some people think that means trouble comes to the just like it does to the unjust.[17] Un uh! No, no, that's not what it means. Rain's a blessin'. Bible's saying God pours out this blessin' on even the unjust. He's hoping they'll see His goodness and call on Him.[18] But here I am just a ramblin'. Tell me what you two are doing."

"First," Jason said, "where is Leroy? How's he doing?"

"He's off on his bicycle, visiting some young folk on the street behind us. He'll sure be sorry he missed seeing you. He says he's going to see his friend, Freddy, but Freddy's got a pretty little sister named Samantha. She's just one year younger than Leroy. I don't pry. I don't have to. He talks about her more than he does Freddy. I think he wouldn't mind if Freddy wasn't even there, 'cept it gives him the excuse, you know."

"Well, I sure hope he hasn't had any more trouble with bullies. He's still going to his classes, I guess. I understand O'Shea is still paying for them."

"He is, and God bless Mr. O'Shea! The good Lord oughta bless him good for all he did for us. Those classes have made a world of difference for Leroy. Bullies not bothering him. I think they can tell by his confidence that they'd better leave him alone. Leroy, now, he takes up for other kids when he sees them getting pushed around. Other kids looking up to him, now. Yes, Sir, his world has changed."

"That's music to my ears, Mr. Adams! I love hearing that. I'll make sure Mr. O'Shea knows. How's your daughter, Shirley?"

"Shirley's good. She's good. Having trouble with her car, but other than that, she's good."

"What kind of trouble?" Jason asked.

"You know, first one thing, then another. I guess it's done pretty good, to be as old as it is. It's the same age as Leroy!" At this, he laughed.

"Is it really as old as Leroy?"

"Yes, Sir, sure is. It's held up pretty good till here lately. It goes in and out of the shop. Sometimes Shirley has to ride the bus to work. Bus don't go right by her work, but she walks the four blocks okay. 'Cept when it's raining, then it's tough, you know."

"I wanted you and Leroy to let me know if you needed anything. That applies to Shirley, too. Mr. O'Shea can help with her car." Jason was a little exasperated. [19]

"Mr. O'Shea's already done so much for us, wouldn't seem right to ask for more," Mr. Adams said.

"You just don't know how much Mr. O'Shea gets blessed for doing things for others! I'm sure he would LOVE to help Shirley!" Jenny chimed in.

"Jenny's right, Mr. Adams. It would please him very much to be able to help her."

"Shirley's a good daughter, you know. Been good to me and Leroy. We usually ride the bus to church of a Sunday morning, then again Sunday night. Bus has been broke for a while, so Shirley's been coming by to take us, only when her car is broke, too, none of us gets to go. Shirley belongs to a different church, but she goes to ours when she has to take us. Been kinda nice to have her settin' by me in church, to tell the truth. We missed today. Didn't none of us get to go."

Jason was thinking that O'Shea needed to see about the church bus, as well as buy Shirley a new car. "What church do you go to?" he asked Adams.

"It's the AME over on Union Street. Not too big, but it's got a lot of good folks. Preacher's good, too. Been going there all my adult life. I was raised in church. Doin' the same with Leroy."[20]

Jason could send O'Shea's check for Shirley's car to Mr. Adams's house, and now he knew where to check on the church bus and where to send the check, if it was needed, as it appeared to be.

Jason and Jenny visited a while longer with Mr. Adams, then told him "goodbye" so they could continue home.

"Tell Leroy we were sorry we didn't get to see him, but we were glad to hear he's doing so well. We'll tell Mr. O'Shea about Shirley's car, so you'll be hearing from him," Jason said.

"I'm so glad I got to meet you, Mr. Adams," Jenny said, as she gave him a hug. She and Jason were both excited as they talked on the way home about what they could do for Shirley and for the AME church.

"I'm sure glad we stopped by there," Jason said. "They weren't going to let me know they had this need. I'm glad God nudged me to go see them. I'm trying to be more sensitive to His nudges."[21]

CHAPTER FIVE

Wounded Veteran

It had been nearly three weeks since Jason and Mr. Allewine had asked the Sheriff to fire Luther Hall. Jason knew it would take some time for the proper procedures to be carried out, so he hadn't spent too much time thinking about it. He and Jenny had prayed for Luther, since he certainly didn't seem to have a God-like character and appeared to be unsaved.[22]

He and Jenny both felt that Hell was too terrible a destiny to wish on anybody and hoped that Luther would meet Jesus and have a change of destination.

So, it was a real surprise when his phone rang and the caller ID said "Luther Hall." Luther? Calling him? He answered immediately with a simple "Hello," trying not to show his surprise.

"Is this Jason Lambert?" Luther asked.

"Yes, is this Luther Hall?" He responded.

"Can I talk to you for a minute? That is, if you'll talk to me."

"Sure, Luther. Go ahead. What's on your mind?"

Jason wondered if he was going to ask him to take back his complaint to the Sheriff.

"Well, the Sheriff fired me, like you asked. I sure got called on the carpet. Seems some of the other Deputies had complaints about me, too, and were all in agreement with me being fired. I couldn't find a friend on the Force. Don't have many friends anywhere, I guess."

Jason was surprised at how contrite Luther seemed. He didn't quite know what to say, as he couldn't tell where Luther was going with this. "Go ahead," he said, thinking that was kinda lame, but he didn't know what else to say. He wanted to hear Luther out.

"Well, at first I tried drinking a lot, trying to ease my mind. I didn't want to think about what was happening. Didn't do any good. I just felt worse. I finally wised up and looked at myself in the mirror. 'You really messed up this time, Luther boy,' I told the sorry sight I saw. I guess I had this coming to me. Not guess, I KNOW I had it coming to me. If it hadn't been you, it woulda been somebody else, getting me fired."

"I'm listening, Luther. Go ahead."

"Well, I kinda took stock of myself. 'I'm a better person than this,' I thought. I did alright in the Marines. That's how I got the Deputy job in the first place. My record was good. The war messed me up, though. Can't seem to get it out of my head. Saw two of my buddies get killed, right beside me. Don't know why it didn't get me, too."

When he paused, Jason said, "Keep going, Luther. I'm listening," his voice filled with compassion now. [23] He was seeing a different side of Luther.

"I don't sleep much. Dreams are too bad. Gets real lonely in the middle of the night when you can't sleep. Wife left a year ago. Couldn't take my outbursts of anger, she said. Wanted me to get help. I thought that would be admitting I'm weak. Thought I could do it by myself. Guess I was wrong. Anyway, I got your number from the Police blotter from when I arrested you. Felt like it might do me good to tell you I'm sorry for the way I treated you. I don't see any other way to make amends."[24]

"Luther, thank you for your service to our country in the Marines. The VA has programs to help guys like you returning from the war. Are you in touch with the VA so you can find a program?"

"Yeah, I can go in there and see what they've got. I've heard about those dogs that are trained to help vets. Maybe they can get me one. Heard it could cost as much as $50,000 to get one, though. Always liked dogs. Had one growing up that was like a best buddy."

"Luther, if you're willing to go to the VA and get help, I know a man who would pay for a trained dog for you." Jason was getting excited about seeing a way to help. Cliff O'Shea would LOVE to help a veteran. [25]

"Well, I'll probably go to the VA tomorrow and just see. No place else to go. Nothing else to do. Don't have a job, you know." He gave a little laugh at telling Jason that.

"Yeah, I know," Jason said. "How can I get in touch with you? Where do you live?"

"Got an apartment on Timmons Street. Cobblestone Manor, apartment 3."

"Okay, Luther. Your number's in my Caller ID now. I'll be in touch. I'm serious about getting a dog for you. You wouldn't have to pay a cent. How are you living, since you're not working?"

"Had a little savings. Won't last long, so I'll have to find something I can do pretty quick."

"If you'll get in a program at the VA, the man who will get you a dog will help you financially for a while, too," Jason assured him.

"That sounds awfully good. Don't know that I could ever pay it back, though."

"He wouldn't want you to pay it back. He loves helping people," Jason said. "Let me know what the VA says tomorrow, okay?"

"Okay. I feel some better, just telling you I'm sorry about the way I treated you, and Jason, you probably did me a favor getting me fired. Made me face up to the fact that I need help. Not so macho after all, I guess."

"There's not really a Superman anywhere. We all need help sometime.[25] It's just hard to admit it. I really appreciate the fact that you called and apologized.

That took some courage. Call me tomorrow after the VA. Okay?"

"Yeah. I will. Thank you, Jason."

Jason couldn't wait to tell Jenny. They would keep praying for Luther, and now Jason knew he would get the chance to talk to him about Jesus as well as help him financially.[26]

CHAPTER SIX

Brent Austin

One day Jason was at the school, trying to figure out how to find the culprits who were taking cell phones and IPads from lockers. The students all had combination locks for their lockers, so the cell phones and IPads should be safe and secure when placed there. The problem was, not wanting to dial the combination each time they had to go to the locker and get a book for the next class, many of the students had resorted to just making the lock look like it was closed when it actually was still open. This made it easy for a thief to take whatever was inside. Usually, the items taken would turn up in the Lost and Found a month or so later, but the theft would have caused many problems in the meantime.

He couldn't just fingerprint every student and find the culprit that way, so he had to find a solution. He was just walking in the hall and praying for guidance when a boy approached him and asked, "Can I talk to you a minute?" He looked a little familiar, but Jason realized he didn't really know him. Probably had just seen him in the halls, he reasoned. There were hundreds of students, and though Jason knew a lot of them by name, this was not one he had spent any time with. At least, he didn't think so.

"Sure thing!" Jason enthusiastically answered, placing a hand on the boy's shoulder. "My office is right down the hall. Are you free this period?"

"Study Hall," the boy replied. "I finished the homework I needed to do and got excused to go to the bathroom."

Jason pulled out a chair for the boy, then sat casually on top of his desk facing him as he asked, "What's on your mind? Everything going okay?"

"You don't remember me, I guess. I've been thinking about talking to you for a while. I see you in the halls all the time, talking to kids," the boy started. He was clearly uncomfortable, but he had initiated the conversation, so he must have something he really wanted to talk about.

"You do look a little familiar. So we've met before?" Jason asked.

"Yeah. I mean, yes, Sir. I was one of the group aggravating a little black boy a while back. You broke it up, and you made me see how bad it looked. I've been pretty ashamed of what we were doing ever since. I would apologize to the boy if I ever saw him again." The boy looked up at Jason, a pleading look on his face.

Jason reached out and put a hand on his shoulder. "I'm glad to hear it. What's your name?"

"Brent. Brent Austin. I'm not hanging out with that gang anymore.[27] They were just the first ones who were friendly to me when I moved here."

"Where did you move from?" Jason asked.

"Tennessee. I had lived in a small town there all my life till my dad got moved here with his job. The move was kinda hard." Brent looked down at his hands as he said this. "This school is so big."

"You felt kinda lost, I guess," Jason offered.

"Yeah. Lost is a good word. It's hard, not knowing anybody. Everybody else seemed to know where to go. They all had friends. Felt like I was the only one that didn't fit in. Those other guys were kinda friendly to me, so I just did what they did. It didn't feel good, though."

"I understand. We're trying to prevent situations like that now. When we have someone new enroll, we assign another student to them to get them acclimated. Once they're settled in and have some friendships, they don't need that guide anymore," Jason explained.

"That's good," Brent said.

Brent got up to leave, saying, "I've just wanted to tell you that the way you saw me that day is not the way I am. I don't mistreat people. I'm sorry for what we did that day."

"I'm glad to hear it, Brent, and I believe you. It took courage for you to come tell me this. I admire that." Jason had slid off his desk, and now he put his hand on Brent's shoulder again. "Maybe you could help us when we have other new students. You know, be a friend to them until they can make friends on their own."

"I'd like that," Brent said. "I know my way around now. There are a lot of things about this school that I really like. I'm beginning to be glad we moved here."

"Hmmm. Sounds to me like there could be a girl involved!" Jason teased.

Brent laughed. "Yeah, and some other friends I've made at church. It's all pretty good, now."

"I'm glad," Jason added. "Thanks for coming to talk to me. I'll look you up as soon as a new student enrolls, okay?"

"Okay, and thanks." Brent was smiling now as he shook the hand Jason was offering.

As he left, Jason thought, "That gang he was hanging out with, the ones who were harassing Leroy Adams, I need to learn their names and watch them. They might be the ones behind the thefts from the lockers." He headed to Ms. Benson's office to discuss it with her.

CHAPTER SEVEN

Lots of Needs

Ms. Benson was chewing on the end of a pencil and looking out the window when Jason knocked on her door.

"May I come in?" he asked.

She swung around to look at him and said, "Sure. Come in. Maybe you can help me do some brainstorming and come up with some ideas to fix some things."

"What kind of things?"

"Well," she said, "we've got some very qualified students who can't play on some of the school sports teams because the family can't afford the uniform. Some can't join the band because the family can't afford the instrument. Plus, they would need uniforms, too. People tell me this is just part of life, that I can't fix everything, that I get too emotionally involved in these problems. 'Just be a professional,' they say. 'Just do your job.' But I can't help but be bothered when these kids are so deserving and the problem is not their fault. So there, Mr. Fixit. What do you say? Are you going to tell me the same thing?"

"Noooo," he said slowly. "My philosophy is that for every problem there is a solution.[28] That means there is a solution to these problems, and no, I don't think you're too emotionally involved for wanting to help these kids. Tell me, how many kids are we talking about?"

"Dozens," she said. "I could go through the roster and point out some, but what's the use? I don't have the money to buy uniforms or instruments. Anyway, there are probably lots more who haven't spoken up or I don't know about. Probably lots of them would join if the uniform or instrument was free."

She heaved a big sigh and dropped her pencil onto her desk. "So, I guess I should just move on to something I can do something about. Right, Mr. Lambert? How do you advise?"

"Hold on. Hold on," Jason answered. "You're giving up too easily. I have some connections."

"Connections?" she interrupted. "We'd need a Daddy Warbucks or a bunch of friends with deep pockets to fund all of this."

"Well, I would need to know a ballpark figure for the money, and then how to handle it. Would it be an embarrassment to the student for everyone to know he was getting a free uniform or instrument when others had paid for theirs? How can we make it easy for them?"

"I think the coaches could announce that they

had been given an endowment for uniforms, so they would be free to anyone who could make the team," she answered.

"Does that mean we should make ALL of the uniforms free? Even those who can afford to pay would get a free uniform, anyway? Would that be the way to handle it?"

"That might be too costly. I don't know. I guess I'd have to ask each coach to give me an estimate. Band Director, too. But hey, do you REALLY think we could turn up enough money? I'm thinking thousands and thousands. Are your connections that rich?"

"Blessed. My connections are blessed, and they love a good cause. They love helping others.[29] If you can get me a good estimate, I believe it can be done. Now, what else is on your mind while Mr. Fixit is here?"

"That's enough, I think," she laughed. "Well, actually, while you're contacting Daddy Warbucks, there is one particular student I wish we could help. Lee Richardson's a senior. The Counselor just found out that he got kicked out of his home, for what we don't know. He moved in with a friend's family, but got kicked out of there, too. He's not a bad kid, so I can't imagine what's happening. Anyway, he works two fast food jobs and still manages to be a good student. He hasn't been in any trouble here at the school. Right now, he's sleeping in his car."

"So, what can we do for him? How can we help?"

"Well, getting him a furnished apartment would almost take a miracle, but it's what he really needs. Most apartment complexes won't rent to an 18-year-old, even if he had the money. If WE had the money, our Counselor could pay the Security Deposit and a few months' rent, till school's out. He'll graduate and should be able to get a better job with his High School diploma, so he won't have to work two jobs any longer. That's a good bit of money, though. I don't happen to have it under my mattress," she said with a wry smile.

"Your wish is my command. I'll make some contacts. With that, I'll bid you farewell."

He had his hand on the doorknob and was about to leave when he remembered what he had come to her office for. "I have a wish list of my own," he said and turned back to his chair.

"When I first came here and interviewed with you, I went to buy gas and found five white boys aggravating a little black boy. I broke it up and followed up with the black boy, but I didn't get the names of the boys who were causing the trouble. A boy named Brent Austin just came to talk to me and told me he had been one of the five. He wanted me to know that was not his usual behavior, and he was sorry for what they had done.

"After he left my office, I started thinking that the other four just might be the culprits who are doing the stealing around here. I guess I could look Brent back up and ask him the names of the other four, but he might not feel good about turning the others in. I wish there was another way to handle it."

"Hmm. I remember Brent Austin. He transferred in after the semester had started. Seems like a good kid. I'm surprised he would be caught harassing anyone," Ms. Benson mused.

"I believe he IS a good kid. Said that group was friendly to him when he didn't know anyone else here, so he got caught up in what they were doing. Said he was ashamed of what they had done."

"I can find out from his Home Room teacher who he was hanging out with at first. Maybe we can find the others without involving him," Ms. Benson offered.

"Sounds good. Let me know if you get anywhere with it. If not, we'll have to find another way, or resort to asking Brent. Thanks!"

With that, Jason headed to the Counselor's office to learn what kind of money would be needed to secure an apartment for Lee Richardson. He would talk with Jenny tonight about him and the uniforms and band instruments. They would have to wait until Ms. Benson gave him an estimate from the Coaches and Band Director, but Cliff O'Shea should be able to help Lee Richardson immediately.

CHAPTER EIGHT

Christy's Wedding

Jenny arrived at school a little later than usual. When she had started out the door, the heavy downpour sent her running back to find an umbrella. It took a few minutes, then she had to drive slower because of the wet roads. She always liked to arrive earlier than she had to so she could get organized before the students came in, and she liked to be there in case a student was waiting to talk to her. This happened fairly often, she had found.

Today it wasn't a student waiting to see her, but her friend Christy, the teacher for the Special Needs students.

"Can I talk to you a minute, Jenny?" Christy asked. Of course Jenny wouldn't say "no," but she noticed by the clock that they only had two or three minutes before the students would come pouring into the classroom.

"Sure," Jenny said, "Just let me do something with this wet umbrella."

Christy followed her as she headed to the corner

of the room where the trashcan was. "You know I've been saving all the money I could for about a year now so I could have the wedding of my dreams."

Jenny turned her head sharply to look at Christy's face. "You and Rod haven't broken up, have you?" She looked at Christy with alarm.

"No, no," Christy laughed. "It's nothing like that! I didn't mean to scare you. No, it's something else. You know my dad just got out of the hospital last month after a long stay because of his heart. Well, now the bills are coming in. They're piling up, even after the insurance has paid. Mom and Dad have such a limited income, they don't have much of a margin to pay on something like this. They are really feeling the pressure of these bills. While I was praying for them about this, I felt like the Lord said I should give them the money I've saved for the wedding. Rod and I could still get married with just family, I guess, and that would cost almost nothing. I haven't talked to him about it yet, but I'm sure he would agree. He wasn't crazy about having a big wedding, anyway. That was my idea. I know God is right, and I would love to help my parents, but it's hard to give up on my dream." She had tears in her eyes as she looked to Jenny for a reaction. "You know I'll do what's right. It's just that I've dreamed of my wedding and pictured it so much since I was a little girl."

Jenny hugged her and said, "Christy, your heart

is right, and I'm sure God will bless you for helping your parents."

Just then the students started coming in, so Jenny said, "Let's talk again after school."

Christy just nodded as she turned to leave.

"Cliff O'Shea, have I got an opportunity for you!" Jenny thought as a big smile spread across her face. She did a little dance and clicked her heels, causing several students to give questioning looks. She just smiled at them and told them good morning.

Two days later, Jenny came in to find Christy waiting for her again, all smiles this time. "Jenny! You won't believe this!" she exclaimed. "Look what I found in my box!" She held out a Cashier's check and a note. "Look at this! Someone named Cliff O'Shea gave me a check for $25,000! The note says for all the good I do for the students with special needs, for the way I go the second mile to help them. Jenny, look at this! My wedding money that I gave to my parents was only $13,000. I've got that back and more!"[30]

Jenny managed to look surprised as she pretended to examine the check and the note. "Cliff O'Shea, you say. I've heard of him and of other things like this that he does."

"I don't know him, but I sure would like to. I just called Rod and told him. He laughed and said, 'I guess the big wedding is back on.'"

"Oh, Jenny, God sure is good!"[31]

"Yes, He is, Christy. Yes, He is!" Jenny just smiled.

CHAPTER NINE

Troubled Students

"I've got some names for you, if you'll just stop by my office," Ms. Benson said, leaving a message on Jason's phone. He was talking with a student in his office and had his phone on vibrate. As soon as the student left, he checked his phone and went straight to her office.

"Mrs. Wilson says that she often saw Brent Austin with Butch Ayers, Joe Mitchell, Billy Watson, and Landon Smith when he was first here. Said she had thought it was kinda odd that she never sees them together anymore. I didn't tell her why I was asking. And Jason, there's a common thread connecting those four. All four are in Foster Care. That's not so terribly unusual because about 10% of our students are. Butch Ayers, though, is in his fifth home. Can't seem to stick anywhere. I did a little checking and found that his father is in prison for selling drugs, and I guess his mother just couldn't handle him. I guess he's got a lot of anger built up. He seems to be the leader, Mrs. Wilson said, and the other three are his 'posse.' They seem to look up to him, and they follow his lead."

"Hmm," Jason said, as he digested the information he was just given. "He must be the kinda husky one. I remember one was a good bit bigger than the others. What if we ask Coach Jenkins to see if he can use him on the football team, show a little interest in him, give him some personal contact with a good role model? If he could make the team, he would have a good outlet for his pent-up energy and anger. He must have some leadership ability, since the other three follow him. I'll talk to Jenkins and see what he thinks."

Jason caught Coach Jenkins as he was getting ready for the team's afternoon practice. "Can I talk with you about something for a minute or two, Coach? Won't take long."

"Sure. What's on your mind?"

"There's a student in Mrs. Wilson's homeroom named Butch Ayers. Been in five foster homes, father in prison. He's kinda husky, so he might make a good player for your team. I wondered if you'd seek him out, tell him he looks like a football player, that you need someone his size. Give him a chance. I'm working with Ms. Benson to get some money donated so uniforms could be free. Tell him his is free. I'll see that it's covered. Right now, he's heading in the wrong direction, but we might be in time to get him on a different track. What do you think? Are you willing to give him a try?"

Jason could see that Coach was willing before he even answered. He was shaking his head up and down.

"Yeah. That's the kinda thing I like to do. It worked for a couple of others on the team. Might just work for this one, too. Butch Ayers, you say? Mrs. Wilson's home room? I'll try to catch him tomorrow."

"That would be wonderful! Thank you, Coach. If he doesn't agree to try, or if it just doesn't work out, at least we will have tried. I'll check back with you in a few days to see what you think. Thanks again!"

Jason DID check back about a week later and was thrilled to hear what Coach had to say. "He's a natural! He's strong, and he's a fast learner. It's a little early to see what the final outcome will be, but he actually seems enthused about trying to make the team. He may turn out to be one of my best players! I'll have you to thank," Coach said as he laughed.

"Not only that, but he asked me if there was anything three of his friends could do. I said, 'Sure! We always need more help with the equipment, handling the water, picking up dirty uniforms, etc.' Told him to ask if they would want to do something like that, and the next day, they showed up. They seem willing to work.[32] I told Jesse, the team manager, to show 'em around, teach 'em what to do, so they could help him. He was glad to have the help. We'll see if they keep it up."

"Coach, you have made my day! Your news couldn't

be better! I think I'll bring all my problems to you!"
Jason and the Coach laughed together.

"Gotta get back to work. Keep checking back, Jason.
Anytime you want to."

Jason DID check back, in fact he did it several times.
Every time, the report was good. He felt so much sat-
isfaction that he had found a workable solution.

The intriguing thing was, no more thefts of cell
phones or IPads were reported.

True to her word, Ms. Benson got a figure from all
of the Coaches as to the cost of uniforms. True to HIS
word, Jason approached Cliff O'Shea, his "contact," who
promptly sent a check to the school that completely
covered the cost. He did the same when he had the
figures from the Band Director. To say Ms. Benson
was pleased was a great understatement. She wore a
constant smile for days and days. Jason and Jenny just
smiled smugly.[33]

CHAPTER TEN

Contingency Fund

Jason was out of the school, having something done with his car, one day, so Jenny sat down to eat lunch next to Mrs. Morrison, the school Counselor. Jenny realized that though they both had been friendly with each other, she had not gotten to know Mrs. Morrison very well. Now was her chance.

Mrs. Morrison was perfect as a Counselor dealing with children. In her fifties, she was plump and matronly, looking like anybody's grandmother. Kids found it easy to confide in her, therefore she knew a ton of things about a bunch of students. After the first few minutes, Jenny was enthralled and transfixed, listening to her. WOW! What an encyclopedia of information! Though she wasn't telling anything that was confidential, she told tales without giving names that Jenny found touching and fascinating.

She told of a student from years ago named Lucy—not her real name, but her real story. Seems Lucy got pregnant when she was seventeen and a senior. She chose to keep the baby. She got some help from her mother, who kept the baby just while Lucy was in school. Lucy realized that if she wanted to provide a good future for her child, she would need a college education. She worked harder than she ever had before, got good grades, and earned a full scholarship to a state college. When she finished, she became an English teacher. She still worked hard, took good care of her daughter, was thrifty, and bought a house for her and her daughter when the girl was in second grade. Then the part that really touched Jenny and captured her interest most of all. Now Lucy was having some financial trouble. She was struggling, so she had taken a job in a clothing store on the weekends. Her mother still kept the daughter while she worked on weekends, but the mother's health was bad, and Lucy didn't know how much longer she would be able to help. The Counselor wasn't telling this to ask for money, but Jenny knew exactly what she and Jason would do. How to learn the teacher's real name, though?

Jenny was fascinated as Mrs. Morrison shared some of the other things she handled for the school that Jenny had never thought of. "Every student is issued a laptop computer to use while in class. They can take them home over the weekend if they pay the $20 insurance for the year. Another $10 and the school can arrange wifi service for them."

"Do most of the students pay this and take the computers home?" Jenny asked.

"Most. We have some whose parents can't afford it, so when I have the money in my 'contingency' fund, I see that it gets covered. I often run out of money, though. We have some really smart kids who could do dual enrollment, get credit from the community college for courses they take with us, if they had the money to pay for the college credit. I try to handle that, too, when I have the funds."

"WOW!" Jenny thought. "What an opportunity to do some good right under our noses!"

"Where do you get the money for your 'contingency' fund?" she asked.

"Different ways. Sometimes a teacher will know of a need of one of her students and will give me the money so that the need is taken care of confidentially. One teacher gave me the money to purchase a lawnmower for a boy to start a lawn care business so he could earn money to help his family. It sometimes seems that there are almost as many needs as there are students!"

Jenny realized that she and Jason could help the teacher who was struggling by giving money to the Counselor and designating it for that teacher, without Jenny having to know the teacher's name. This unknown teacher should be rewarded for keeping her child, for being diligent to get an education that qualified her for a good career job, and for providing a home for her daughter.

That night Jenny shared all she had learned with Jason. "We need to fill up the Counselor's 'contingency' fund, don't you think?" she asked Jason.[34]

"Sure we do. So much need, right under our noses!" Jason said. "I would never have thought of all this. We can give the Counselor most of what's in O'Shea's account now, then the house we bought on the next street over should be ready to sell soon, and should refill OUR 'contingency' fund. Let's see, we bought the house 'as is' for $200,000, and we may owe the contractor and his workers as much as $100,000 for modernizing it and repairing everything. When that's finished, it should sell for $500,000 or more. Even after we pay Tom and his workers, we should clear $200,000 profit, plus get our initial investment of $200,000 back. We'll need to stay in touch with the Counselor and make sure she doesn't run out of funds again!"

CHAPTER ELEVEN

Brother's Surprise

Jenny had put her phone in her pocket, and she felt it vibrate in the middle of the class. She was very involved in the exercise she had the class doing, so she just glanced down to see who was texting. Rick! She would read his message and get back to him as soon as she could.

The class was having a great time doing the lesson Jenny had planned, so much so that they didn't even realize they were learning.

She was teaching Earth Science, but doing it in a novel way. She had divided the class into three groups, had written on several index cards one word in a sentence, then given a card out to each student. Each group had a different sentence. The students in a group had to work together to see that their sentence said something that was true about Earth Science, plus make sure they arranged it with the correct syntax. There was a lot of talking and laughing going on till she called time and had each group read their sentence. The rest of the class could critique each group and decide if the work was correct. This way, each student heard the correct facts, and because it was done in this way, they wouldn't forget it.

She was pleased to see that they were getting it, learning what she was trying to teach.

As soon as the bell rang to end the class, she looked at her phone to see what her brother Rick had to say. He had been deployed right after her wedding, so she hadn't seen him in quite a while.

He was coming home this weekend! She loved this big brother with all her heart, and they had a very special bond. He had been eleven when their father had been killed in Afghanistan and had felt he had to protect and care for his seven-year-old sister. He had been the perfect big brother.

They had both accepted Ron as their new father when their mother married him, largely because Ron had been careful to develop a relationship with each of them, not just with their mother.

She was smiling as she sent Jason a text: "Rick's coming this weekend!"

Rick was stationed at Norfolk, VA, and his ship had come in three weeks earlier. The family knew his ship had come in and had expected to see him the next day or so, but Mom had received a message from him that he had something to take care of in Norfolk before he came home. Now he was coming in two days!

In his text to Jenny, he asked if she and Jason would

be at Mom and Dad's around noon on Saturday. "Must have something up his sleeve that he wants to surprise us with," Jenny thought. "I bet he's been promoted again!"

Saturday was a beautiful day as the four of them waited anxiously. They had eaten lunch, cleared the dishes away, looked out the window a dozen times, and waited some more. It was only a few minutes after one, still Rick was always very punctual, so they kept looking.

Finally, his car pulled into the yard, and all four rushed out to greet him. Whoa! The first person to get out of the car was a little four-year-old boy, while Rick sat smiling through the windshield. He apparently enjoyed their look of astonishment.

Within seconds he was out of the car, hugging his mom, then each of the others. The little boy stood by the car, smiling hesitantly.

"I've got somebody I want you to meet," Rick smiled as he placed his hand on the little boy's shoulder. "This is Joey, and ...." He opened the car door. "And this is Lisa, his mom."

A pretty young girl stepped out of the car, smiling shyly and looking almost too young to be the mother of the boy.

"Mom, Dad, Sis, Jason, this is my fiancee', and Joey is going to be my son. Lisa has agreed to marry me!"[35] When Mom finally found her voice, she said, "Well, welcome Lisa, and you, too, Joey. What a wonderful surprise!"

"Congratulations, Son!" Dad shook his hand, then hugged him again.

"You've never been good at keeping secrets. How did you keep this from us?" Jenny asked as she put a hand on the boy's shoulder and smiled broadly at his mom.

"She just agreed! You're knowing it almost as soon as I am!" Rick explained that they had been dating before his deployment and had facetimed every day that they could while he was gone. He had known he wanted to marry her for some time now, but she hadn't said "yes" until his deployment was over. The facetimes had included Joey, and Rick had asked him to work on his mother to get her to agree to marry him. "Joey did a good job, so she said 'yes'."

"Well, welcome again, Lisa," Mom said as she hugged the girl who had hardly said a word, then Mom stooped down in front of Joey to say, "And you, young man, will be my first grandchild. That means you are very special! Welcome to you, too!" Then she gave him a hug, too.

Jason had just been watching the entire scene, smiling and shaking his head. Now he said, "Welcome, Lisa and Joey. You're getting a great guy there." Then turning to Rick, "You can go on keeping secrets and surprising us, as long as the surprises are as good as this!"

"Come on inside," Mom said. "Have you had lunch? Can I fix you something to eat?" as she led the way into the house.

"We had a late breakfast," Rick explained. "But I would like some of your wonderful tea. Lisa, Joey, are you hungry?"

"Just tea for me, too, and maybe milk for Joey," Lisa said, as they went inside.

As they sat around the table, Mom said to Rick, "You never fail to amaze me, but you outdid yourself this time!"

"Well, Mom, Lisa is the most wonderful girl I've ever met, and to get Joey in the bargain, well, you can see why I persisted until she said 'yes'."

Jenny sat next to Joey and refilled his milk glass when he needed it. She was so happy for Rick, but it was a lot to take in. She would be an instant Aunt. How would she do in that role? And they would probably live in Norfolk, so she would have to get to know Lisa and Joey on a long-distance basis. She was already thinking of things she would buy for Joey. And Lisa would be her sister. She had always wanted one, and surely Rick had picked one who would fit perfectly into the family.

"Joey's dad was killed in an accident two years ago," Rick explained. "Lisa has done a wonderful job as a single mom. Now I want to help her do that job. I know we can become a real family because you showed me the way, Dad," he said to Ron. This brought tears to Ron's eyes. He just nodded and reached out and took Mom's hand.[36]

"Are you guys staying tomorrow, too? Maybe we could take Joey to the park. Maybe even have a picnic," Jason ventured.

"We can stay till Wednesday," Rick answered. "Lisa took some days off from her job, and I have two weeks of leave. We'll come back down next weekend, too."

The longer they all talked, the more comfortable Lisa and Joey seemed. There were so many questions to ask. So much to learn.

"WOW! How life has suddenly changed. More family to love," Jenny thought. "Thank you, God, for these two sweet, wonderful people being added to our family."

CHAPTER TWELVE

Sadie Moore

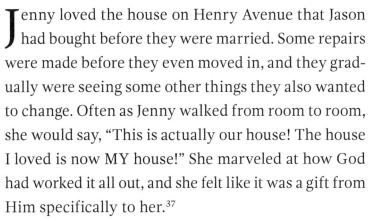

Jenny loved the house on Henry Avenue that Jason had bought before they were married. Some repairs were made before they even moved in, and they gradually were seeing some other things they also wanted to change. Often as Jenny walked from room to room, she would say, "This is actually our house! The house I loved is now MY house!" She marveled at how God had worked it all out, and she felt like it was a gift from Him specifically to her.[37]

It now had a new roof, and some shutters had been repaired and painted the "Robin's-Egg-Blue" color Jenny loved. Just looking at it each afternoon as she drove into the driveway put her in a really happy mood.

She loved every nook and cranny and never tired of just exploring from room to room, making mental notes of small changes she wanted to make. She and Jason had agreed that they would take out the wall between the living and dining rooms to make a great room, so the repairmen were coming on Saturday to do just that.

The wallpaper in the dining room was obviously from a different era, and Jenny wanted to keep a square-foot piece to frame and hang in the foyer. She wanted to salvage this piece before the repairmen began demolition. One spot looked like it had been covered over with a picture, as it was more vivid than all around it. The rest didn't look so faded, until you compared it with this spot. She measured and marked the piece she wanted, cutting it carefully with a box cutter. Funny. The blade seemed to fall into a groove as she cut. Obviously, this section of the wall had been cut before.

Another layer of wallpaper was behind the first, so the people who hung this wallpaper hadn't bothered to remove the previous one. The glue that held the layers of wallpaper to the wall had long ago dried and deteriorated so that the layers easily peeled away when she carefully tugged at a corner.

As she pulled them away from the plaster wall beneath, she was surprised to see that her blade had indeed been cutting into a groove that was around the square-foot piece. This groove went all the way through the plaster and then the boards behind it. A perfect square cut through the wood. How strange! What could be behind it?

Carefully she pried the wood out with the blade of her box cutter.

There in front of her was a stack of a dozen or

more letters, yellowed with age, tied up with a coarse brown string.[38] Her heart was pounding as she lifted the bundle out into the light so she could read the address. "Miss Sadie Moore" she read, then the very street address where she and Jason now lived. She gingerly thumbed through the entire stack and saw the name and address of each one was the same.

Not a single one had been opened.

What had she stumbled upon? What could this mean? Letters that had never been read? She counted thirteen in all.

She couldn't wait for Jason to come home so she could show him what she had found. When she showed him, he was as puzzled as she had been. Then they both became excited. Maybe they could find Miss Sadie Moore, if she was still living.

He looked through his desk until he found the contact information for the Andrews, the elderly couple he had bought the house from.

"I believe it WAS a Moore family we bought the house from," Mr. Andrews said. "I don't think they're still living, though. They were pretty old, and that was many years ago. Let me ask Eva if she remembers anything about them that would help you." Jason could hear him lay the phone down and heard his shuffling gait as he went to another room to find his wife.

Several moments later, he was back on the phone. "I'll put Eva on in a minute, and you can ask her. You say you and your wife are living in the house. Does it suit you? Is it working for you? Do you like it?"

"Like it? We LOVE it! Turns out my wife had been admiring it when she drove through the area, and she had a hard time believing I had bought it. We love everything about it. We're about to remove the wall between the living room and dining room to make a great room, and Jenny wanted to save a piece of the wallpaper. When she cut the piece out, she found the wood behind it had been cut out and placed back, then behind the wood she found some letters. They've never been opened, and we wondered if we could get them to a family member."

"Well, I'll be. A secret spot. Then with wallpaper over it, we never knew it was there. Well, here's Eva. She might remember something about the family."

When Jason had explained about the letters to Mrs. Andrews, she thought a minute, then said, "Seems like I do remember there was an old maid sister living with the Moores. I think they're both dead, but the sister was a little younger. Maybe she's still living. Probably in a Nursing Home somewhere. If you check around, you might find her or somebody who knows whether she's alive or not. I'm not much help, I'm afraid."

"No, you've been a great help. We'll check around. And, by the way, we love the house. Maybe we'll live in it as long as you did. Thank you, Mrs. Andrews. God bless you two. Stay well." With that, Jason hung up.

He turned to Jenny, who was waiting anxiously to know what he had learned. "You've got some sleuthing to do, young lady. There was an old maid sister living with the Moores. She might be our Sadie. She might be in a Nursing Home nearby, if she's still living." Jason smiled to see the excited look on Jenny's face.

"Jason, we've got to find her. Don't look so smug! You're excited about it, too, you big lug." She playfully punched him on the shoulder.

"Well, get to work!" he said, as he handed her the phone.

Jenny was thinking this might take forever, but she had to try. She couldn't believe her luck when the secretary at the fifth Nursing Home said, "Yes, we do have a Sadie Moore. I believe she's in the Day Room right now, so she's not near a phone. May I give her a message? Are you a relative?"

"No, we're not related, but I believe we may have found something that belonged to her. Are we allowed to visit now? What are your hours?" Jenny asked.

"We lock the place down at 9PM. Come any time until then," was the answer.

Jenny did a little dance as she hung up the phone. This time it was Jason who was waiting anxiously to hear what SHE had learned.

"Jason, can we go right now? It's just over on Cleaver Street. Please, can we go now? Please?"

He just stood there, grinning to tease her, but he

quickly moved when she grabbed her purse and the letters and headed for the door. "You really meant right now, didn't you?"

The Day Room had about eight people in wheelchairs scattered about. The attendant who was packing up the Bingo cards pointed to the little lady slumped in a wheelchair by the window. Jenny felt like she was in a dream, that this couldn't be real, that she had actually found the person to whom the letters were addressed.

She stood quietly beside the chair for a minute before she spoke, not wanting to startle the fragile-looking little woman who was wrapped in a shawl, her knees covered with a lap robe. When Jenny looked in her face, she saw the eyes were open but they looked glazed, as if she were seeing but not seeing.

"Miss Moore?" she asked.

"Huh? Yes. Who is it?" Her voice was almost too low to be heard.

"Miss Sadie Moore? I'm Jenny Lambert. May I talk with you for a few minutes?" Jenny stooped in front of the wheelchair so she could be seen.

Sadie straightened up in the chair a bit, and her eyes seemed to clear as she looked at Jenny. "You're a pretty young thing," she said.

"Thank you," Jenny said. "This is my husband, Jason," as she nodded to Jason, who was standing behind her.

"Hello, Miss Moore," Jason said. "I'm very happy to meet you."

Sadie turned her head a bit to look at Jason and gave a slight nod.

"We live in a house on Henry Avenue that we believe you once lived in," Jenny started. She was trying to figure out how to tell her about the letters.

"Henry Avenue. Yes, I lived there for years. You say you live there now? I lived with my parents. When they died, my brother and his wife moved in, and I stayed with them. They're all gone now. All gone but me. I'm the last survivor of my family."

"I found some letters that had been hidden in a wall. They have never been opened. They're addressed to Miss Sadie Moore," Jenny said, as she pulled the stack of letters from her purse.

"Letters? To me? I don't remember any letters." Sadie spoke slowly, looking out the window. "Who are they from?"

"Ensign Meyer Goldstein, and some from Lieutenant JG Meyer Goldstein."

Sadie turned her head quickly to look down at the letters. She was more alert now. She sat up straight. "Meyer? Letters from Meyer? But Meyer never wrote to me." She reached out to touch the letters, her hand trembling. "You sure they're from Meyer?"

"That's what the return address says on each one.

There are thirteen of them." Jenny lifted them up and placed them in Sadie's hand.

Tears now filled Sadie's eyes and began to trickle down her wrinkled cheeks. She held the letters for a while, not saying a word. Then, "Letters from Meyer. Meyer wrote letters to me. Meyer DID write to me. He DIDN'T forget me!" Now a sob escaped from her mouth, as she lifted the packet and softly kissed the top letter. "Oh, Meyer. Oh, Meyer. You DID write to me. I never knew. I thought you had moved on and forgotten me."

Jenny was now crying, too, and she heard Jason behind her clear his throat. She reached and grabbed Sadie's other hand. The thought of what must have happened was too terrible to imagine.

"They hid his letters from me," she said slowly as if she was now realizing what had happened. "Poor Mama and Papa. They thought they were protecting me. That's what they said when they wanted me to stop seeing him." Another sob escaped. "Poor Mama and Papa. Oh, Meyer. You didn't forget me. You didn't FOR-GET me. You wrote me letters. Letters from Meyer." Her voice trailed off.

"Miss Sadie, I'm so sorry. If you need help reading, I could read them to you," Jenny offered.

"No, that's alright. I use a magnifying glass, but I can read. Mama and Papa were wrong, you know. They wanted me to forget Meyer. Said I would meet someone else who was 'better suited' for me. They were wrong. I had given my heart to Meyer. I never met anyone else I cared for. Never."

She was looking out the window again, with a far-away look, looking back over the years. She held the packet of letters against her heart.

"Miss Sadie, would you want us to see if we could track Meyer down? To see if he's still living? Maybe he is. Maybe we could find him." Jenny's voice was hopeful, excited at the idea.

"Find Meyer? I don't know. Do you think you could? All these years. Do you think it's possible?" Miss Sadie's face brightened a bit.

"Miss Sadie, there must be some reason why I found those letters when I did. God must have led me to that hiding place in the wall. Then He let us find you." Jenny was sounding more confident, was being persuasive. She looked back at Jason, wondering if she was going too far. Wouldn't it be bad to get Miss Sadie's hopes up, then find that Meyer had long been dead? "What do you think, Jason?" she asked.

"I think we need to pray about it and get God's guidance. That is, if Miss Sadie agrees." Jason looked questioningly at Miss Sadie and waited for her answer.

END OF BOOK 3

Leaders' Guide

1 Seek God's guidance. *"In all your ways, acknowledge Him, and He shall direct your paths"* (Prov. 3:6).

2 Life begins at conception: *"Before I formed you in the womb I knew you"* (Jer. 1:5a).

3 God has good plans for each of us. *"For I know the thoughts that I think toward you, says the Lord, thoughts of peace and not of evil, to give you a future and a hope"* (Jer. 29:11).

4 We are commanded not to murder. *"You shall not murder"* (Ex. 20:13).

5 God's ways are higher than ours. *"For as the heavens are higher than the earth, so are My ways higher than your ways"* (Isa. 55:9a).

6 Peace. *"And the peace of God, which surpasses all understanding, will guard your hearts and minds through Christ Jesus"* (Phil. 4:7).

7 Seek God's guidance. *"In all your ways, acknowledge Him, and He shall direct your paths"* (Prov. 3:6).

8 God wants us to ask Him for help when we need it. *"Let us therefore come boldly to the throne of*

grace, that we may obtain mercy and find grace to help in time of need" (Heb. 4:16).

9 Good Samaritan. *"But a certain Samaritan, as he journeyed, came where he was. And when he saw him, he had compassion. So he went to him and bandaged his wounds, pouring on oil and wine; and he set him on his own animal, brought him to an inn, and took care of him"* (Lk 10:33-34).

10 God can bring good out of any situation. *"And we know that all things work together for good to those who love God, to those who are called according to His purpose"* (Rom. 8:28).

11 Be persistent. *"So I say to you, ask, and it will be given to you; seek, and you will find; knock, and it will be opened to you"* (Lk 11:9).

12 We are to share the Gospel everywhere we go. *"And He said to them, 'Go into all the world and preach the gospel to every creature'"* (Mk 16:15).

13 Don't tell lies. *"You shall not bear false witness against your neighbor"* (Ex 20:16).

14 In everything give thanks. *"In everything give thanks, for this is the will of God in Christ Jesus for you"* (1 Thes. 5:18).

15 Laughter is good medicine. *"A merry heart does good like a medicine, but a broken spirit dries the bones"* (Prov. 17:22).

16 Do good when you can. *"Do good, and lend, hoping for nothing in return, and your reward will be great, and you will be sons of the Most High"* (Lk 6:35b).

17 God blesses even the unjust. *"He makes His sun rise on the evil and the good, and sends rain on the just and the unjust"* (Matt 5:45).

18 The goodness of God leads men to repentance. *"Or do you despise the riches of His goodness forbearance, and longsuffering, not knowing that the goodness of God leads you to repentance"* (Rom 2:4)?

19 Do a thorough job of what you do. *"Whatever your hand finds to do, do it with your might"* (Ecc. 9:10a).

20 Children need to be raised in church. *"Train up a child in the way he should go, and when he is old he will not depart from it"* (Prov. 22:6).

21 God speaks in a still, small voice. *"... the Lord was not in the wind; and after the wind, an earthquake, but the Lord was not in the earthquake; and after the earthquake a fire, but the Lord was not in the fire; and after the fire, a still, small voice. And so it was, ... Elijah heard it"* (1 Kings 19:11b-13a).

22 Pray for your enemies. *"But I say to you, love your enemies, bless those who curse you, do good to those*

*who hate you, and pray for those who spitefully use
you and persecute you"* (Matt 5:44).

23 Forgive! *"For if you forgive men their trespass-
es, your heavenly Father will also forgive you"*
(Matt 6:14).

24 Make amends if you can. *"Therefore if you bring
your gift to the altar, and there remember that your
brother has something against you, leave your gift
there before the altar, and go your way. First be
reconciled to your brother and then come and offer
your gift"* (Matt 5: 23-24).

25 Help each other. *"Bear one another's burdens, and
so fulfill the law of Christ"* (Gal 6:2).

26 Overcome evil with good. *"Do not be overcome by
evil, but overcome evil with good"* (Rom. 12:21).

27 Stay away from bad company. *"My son, if sinners
entice you, do not consent. ... My son, do not walk in
the way with them, keep your foot from their path;
for their feet run to evil"* (Prov 1:10, 15-16a).

28 Faith can do what is humanly impossible. *"...
if you have faith as a mustard seed, you will say
to this mountain, 'Move from here to there,' and it
will move; and nothing will be impossible for you"*
(Matt 17:20).

29 The giver is blessed! *"And remember the words of*

the Lord Jesus, that He said, 'It is more blessed to give than to receive'" (Acts 20:35b).

30 Honor your parents. *"Honor your father and mother, which is the first commandment with promise: that it may be well with you and you may live long on the earth"* (Eph. 6:2).

31 God is good! *"Praise the Lord! O give thanks to the Lord, for He is good! His mercy endures forever"* (Ps 106:1).

32 Be willing to work. *"Whatever your hand finds to do, do it with your might"* (Ecc 9:10a).

33 Give your gift in secret. *"But when you do a charitable deed, do not let your left hand know what your right hand is doing, that your charitable deed may be in secret, and your Father who sees in secret will Himself reward you openly"* (Matt 6: 3-4).

34 When you see a need and are able to meet it, you must do so. *"If a brother or sister is naked and destitute of daily food, and one of you says to them, 'Depart in peace, be warmed and filled,' but you do not give them the things which are needed for the body, what does it profit?"* (James 2:15).

35 It is not good to be alone. *"And the Lord God said, 'It is not good that man should be alone"* (Gen. 2:18a).

36 It is not good to be alone. *"God sets the solitary in families"* (Ps 68:6a).

37 When we please God, He pleases us. *"Delight yourself also in the Lord, and He shall give you the desires of your heart"* (Ps 37:4).

38 God will show us hidden things. *"And I will give you the treasures of darkness and hidden riches of secret places, that you may know that I, the Lord, who call you by your name, am the God of Israel"* (Isa 45:3).

CPSIA information can be obtained
at www.ICGtesting.com
Printed in the USA
BVHW030533211121
622154BV00001B/65